# The Magical Worry Balloon

## Bedtime Healing Meditation for Children

Little Blue Zen

# THE MAGICAL WORRY BALLOON

## Copyright@ 2024 Jo Galloway

The right of the author has been asserted to her following the copyright writing, designs and patent act of Australia.

All rights reserved. No part of this book may be reproduced, stored or transmitted by any means whether auditory, graphic, mechanical, or electronic without the written permission of the author. Unauthorised reproduction of any part of this work is illegal and is punishable by law.

Unless otherwise noted, the author and the publisher make no explicit guarantees as the accuracy of the information contained in this book may differ based on individual experiences and context

ISBN: 978-1-7635801-2-1

Published by Little Blue Zen
Birdwood NSW
Printed in Australia
Cover Design: Gagan Karunachandra
Editing: Kristine Gibson
jo@littlebluezen.com
http://www.littlebluezen.com

# The Magical Worry Balloon

## Bedtime Healing Meditation for Children

Jo Galloway

**Your child may like other books in
this series**

- Bully Proof. Keeping out the bullies.

- A Coat of Flying Colours. Passing your Exams.

- The Magical Treasure Hunt. Building Confidence.

- I am Different, I am Me.

- Angelic Dreams. Meet your Guardian Angel.

- Scared of the Dark.

- I Love School.

- Bedwetting. Dry Nights.

# INTRODUCTION

## Why Healing Meditations.

As children we make sense of our experiences based on our limited understanding and perception. We may misinterpret events or draw conclusions that form the basis of limiting beliefs that influence our entire life. These beliefs become ingrained over time, shaping our thoughts, feelings and behaviours well into adulthood unless consciously challenged.

In my work as a practising Hypnotherapist, I've found that all my clients' concerns, whether rooted in fears, feelings of inadequacy, addictive behaviours, or other challenges, trace back to their early childhood experiences, interactions, and upbringing. It's important to note that these issues don't exclusively stem from abusive or dysfunctional environments; limiting beliefs can arise from various circumstances.

Parents or caregivers wield substantial influence in shaping our perceptions of ourselves and the world around us. Remarks, criticisms, or comparisons made by family members can foster beliefs about our capabilities, worthiness, or potential. Furthermore, interactions with peers, teachers, and authority figures also contribute to the formation of these beliefs. Repeated experiences of rejection or failure can solidify beliefs such as "I'm not good enough" or "I'm unworthy of love."

This realzsation ignited my passion for intervening at the source: working with children to prevent these beliefs from taking root and manifesting into significant challenges in adulthood. By addressing issues early on, we can guide children to develop into the best versions of themselves, free from the burden of limiting beliefs that could otherwise dominate their lives.

.

## How Healing Meditation will help your child.

Teaching children meditation offers a multitude of benefits that can positively influence their daily lives and overall development. A regular mindfulness meditation practice provides valuable tools for managing stress, navigating emotions, and promoting overall well-being. Healing meditations, in particular, bolster your child's self-belief, helping to remove any resistance they may face in adulthood. This leads to a happier, more successful and fulfilling life.

Unlike traditional meditation, which often centres on relaxation, healing meditations go a step further by focusing on recovery, balance, and reprogramming a child's self-belief. These meditations use techniques such as breathing exercises, visualization, and guided imagery to not only foster deep relaxation but also reshape their mindset.

This targeted approach helps build a stronger sense of self-confidence and resilience. By integrating positive affirmations and emotional healing, healing meditations offer a distinct advantage over traditional methods, laying a powerful foundation for a child's future success and well-being.

Meditation can also be an effective part of your child's bedtime routine, helping to calm the mind and prepare the body for restful sleep. Techniques like guided imagery and deep breathing, as outlined in this book, can signal to the brain that it's time to wind down.

Sharing these calming moments at bedtime not only strengthens the bond between parent and child, but also creates a supportive and nurturing environment. It also sets a positive example, emphasizing the importance of self-care and mindfulness.

With patience and consistency, you can help your child develop a lifelong practice that supports their mental, emotional, and physical health. Give your child the gift of relaxation and imagination with this easy-to-read story designed to inspire and uplift.

# The Magical Worry Balloon

Embark on a magical adventure with "The Magical Worry Balloon"! Follow your child on a journey to a mountaintop where imagination knows no bounds. There, they discover a breathtaking hot air balloon adorned in every colour of the rainbow. Attached to its basket is a sign that reads, "Leave all your worries here."

As each worry is gently placed into the basket, your little one begins to feel lighter, freer and more confident. With the balloon soaring higher and higher, carried by the gentle breeze, it carries away all their worries and fears, leaving behind a peaceful sense of calm.

Through this enchanting tale, children learn the empowering lesson of letting go of worries and embracing positivity. As they drift off to sleep, they carry with them the assurance that they can always return to the mountain and the magical balloon whenever they need to.

"The Magical Worry Balloon" is a heartwarming story that promises sweet dreams filled with hope for a brighter tomorrow. Delivered in a slow, monotone voice, this story captivates and soothes. THE MAGICAL WORRY BALLOON is also available on YouTube, providing a soothing auditory experience for children seeking comfort and empowerment.

**Listen on YouTube**

# The Magical Worry Balloon

Hello, my Little Starlight.

Are you ready to go on a magical adventure?

Before we set off, let's take a big, long stretch.

Stretch out your arms and legs, stretch your fingers and toes.

Oh, doesn't that feel so good!

Have a little wiggle, and when you're ready, lying nice and still, softly close your eyes.

Did you know you can see perfectly well with your eyes closed?

Because all boys and girls have the most amazing ability to see things way better than grownups can.

This is called your imagination.

So, let's get started by focusing on your breathing.

Take a slow, deep breath in.

Notice how your belly rises as you breathe in.

And as you breathe out, your belly goes down.

You go up and down with every breath you take.

Let's try it again: breathe in, belly rises up, then breathe out, belly goes down.

Wow, you are doing amazingly well.

Let's do that one more time, shall we?

Take a nice, deep, slow breath in, pushing your belly up.

Then breathe out slowly as your belly goes down, like a balloon letting go of all its air.

Perfect!

Now, as you continue to breathe in and out, feel your body go all loose and floppy.

Floppy like a rag doll.

Your head is getting heavier as it sinks down into your fluffy, soft pillow.

Your feeling ever so sleepy.

Your arms are getting so heavy now.

Your legs are also getting heavier and heavier.

Your bed feels incredibly comfortable.

Wrapped up in a wonderful, loving cuddle, your bed embraces you.

You're feeling very sleepy.

Now, using your brilliant imagination, I want you to imagine that you are standing on top of a mountain.

Feel the sun's warmth on your skin.

If you listen carefully, you can you hear the birds singing in the nearby trees?

Looking down, you can see a field and in this field is a magnificent, magical hot-air balloon.

It is the biggest balloon you have ever seen, and its colours are simply dazzling.

You know this balloon has something incredibly special waiting just for you.

You spot a pathway winding down to the bottom.

Twinkling fairy lights line the path.

This enchanting pathway beckons you, so you happily start walking, following the lights to the field below.

You can see yourself, hear yourself, even feel yourself moving down the pathway.

Filled with excitement to reach the magical balloon, you skip along the path, eager to reach the bottom.

Now you are halfway down the mountain, getting closer and closer to the magical balloon.

The soft noises and sounds you hear are making you feel even sleepier.

There's not much further to go now; you're almost at the bottom.

Your legs are feeling tired and heavy; your arms are feeling heavy too.

Just a few more steps and you will reach the bottom.

Yay, you made it!

Well done, Little Starlight!

Now, you are standing next to the most magnificent hot-air balloon you have ever seen.

The balloon shines brightly, glittering in all the colours of the rainbow.

It floats gracefully above a magical basket.

On the side of the basket, there is a sign that says, **'Leave all your worries here.'** Under the sign is a hole, just like a mailbox. This is where you can leave all your worries, all your unhappy thoughts and feeling.

Sometimes you may have scary thoughts, worries or feelings that make you sad.

This magical basket is where you can leave them.

Even worries about school or going to parties.

You don't want those worries weighing you down.

So, let's say goodbye to them.

Pop them into the letterbox of your special basket.

Now, dig deep... have a look in your pockets.

Make sure you gather all those feelings that make you sad or cranky.

Those feelings that keep you awake, tossing and turning in bed at night.

Place all your worries in the basket.

Do you have worries about not fitting in at school?

Maybe worries that you're not as good as the other kids, or worries about a test you have to take?

Worries about not feeling lovable or important.

Worries because you think you are different.

Place them all in the basket.

Let go of whatever is bothering you.

Put in all your sadness and anger.

Any fears, or sad feelings give them to the worry balloon.

This magical worry balloon is so happy to take all your worries away from you.

Your worries help the balloon fly higher and higher.

The more worries you put in the basket, the faster it can fly and the higher it can go. When the basket becomes full, the wind will pick up the balloon and carry all your worries away.

Those worries are a thing of the past and will never come back.

The balloon loves to take all your worries. Now, check once more that you have placed all your worries into the magical basket.

When you are sure they are all gone, you can lean over and untie the rope that is holding the basket to the ground.

The wind lifts the balloon, carrying with it the basket full of worries.

You step back and watch as the balloon rises higher and higher into the blue sky. Shielding your eyes from the sun, you see the balloon rise over the mountains, taking with it all your worries and sad feelings.

You continue to watch as the balloon fades from sight, drifting off into the distant sky, disappearing into the fluffy white clouds.

Now, all your worries are gone, never to return.

What a fantastic feeling:

Woo hoo.

As you watch the balloon disappear, you notice something special about yourself, something good.

You feel free.

You feel happy.

You're feeling so much better now that you have given all your worries to the magical worry balloon.

You are feeling more confident.

You feel yourself back in control, the captain of your ship.

You feel happier and much calmer.

Feeling carefree, you are ready for anything.

You feel good enough!

The test at school seems like a small thing now because you know how smart, clever, lovable and talented you truly are.

You can do anything you want now that all your worries are gone.

The possibilities are endless - you can be anything you want.

You are good enough, smart enough, and lovable enough.

You are brave, courageous and fearless.

As you feel yourself smiling, you can't resist doing a little happy dance.

You like yourself!

What a great feeling!

You feel amazing.

Now that the wind has carried away all your worries, you know they can never, ever come back.

That feels so good!

You feel excited and can't wait to tell all your friends and family about your special magical worry balloon.

You feel so happy now that all your worries are gone.

Imagine yourself acing your next test at school, making new friends, feeling super brave!

Now, every day you feel calm, confident, totally in control and so happy.

Look at you, with a big smile on your face!

You have thrown away all those old, shy, unwanted feelings and filled yourself up with wonderful, positive feelings.

Now you can really enjoy yourself, woo hoo!

Go You!

You are so clever, amazing and loved.

You know you can come back to visit the mountain anytime you like.

Anytime you have worries, a new empty basket will always be waiting.

No more tossing and turning in bed at night, now that all your worries are gone.

Now you know exactly how calm and confident you truly are, you can gently, calmly, easily drift off to sleep.

You will dream the most magical dreams all the way till the morning light.

Waking up without a worry in the world, feeling happy, calm and safe.

You know you can visit the mountain any time, day or night, whenever you need to, whenever you have worries.

All you have to do is close your eyes, see your magical rainbow balloon and all your worries will disappear, just like magic.

Tomorrow is a brand-new day.
Feeling back in control, you can now easily, peacefully, drift off to sleep.
Good night, my Little Starlight.
Sweet dreams..........

# Also by Jo Galloway

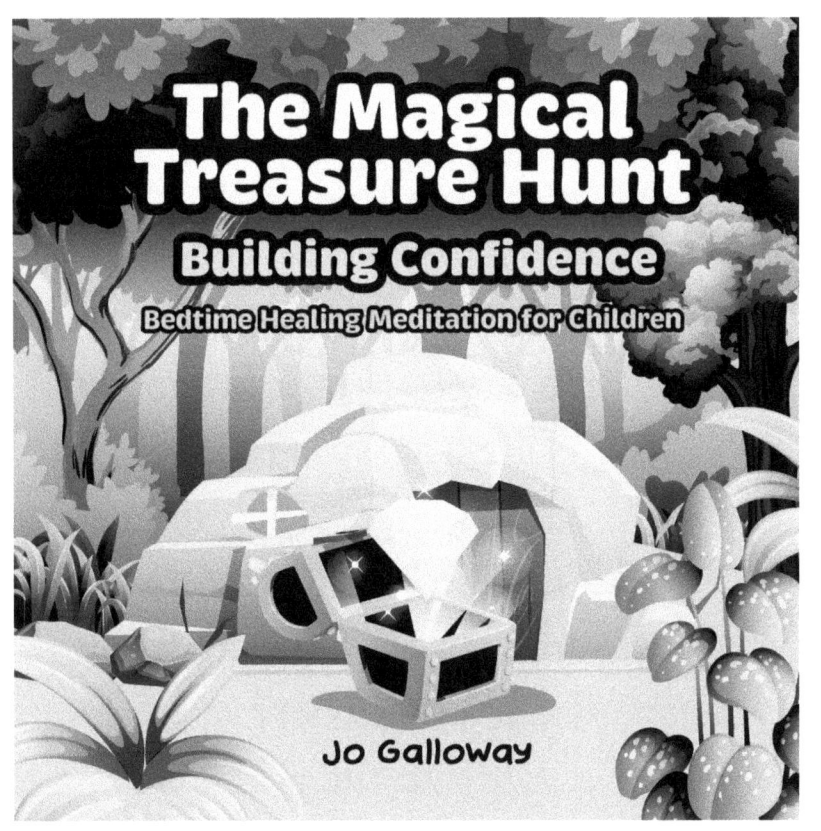

Embark on a whimsical journey with your little one as they venture into the world of self-discovery. As you guide your child through a series of relaxation exercises, they'll descend a rainbow staircase to meet their most cherished friend. Together they travel along an enchanted path. Here they'll uncover glittering stones inscribed with powerful messages: "I am lovable," "My body is beautiful just as it is," "I am good enough," and "I am confident." Each stone is a reminder of their unique strengths and worth, helping them embrace their true selves and shine with self-love and confidence.

# A Coat of Flying Colours

Sitting exams can often bring to the surface a child's self-sabotaging beliefs of I am not good enough, fears of failure or fear of rejection, along with bucket loads of anxiety.

Wearing the magical coat of Flying Colours is like wearing Superman's cape. This coat will transform your child's inner beliefs, allow access to their phenomenal memory, and enable them to remain calm and in total control while undertaking any exam.

Allow this gentle healing meditation to ease their worries, enhance their belief in their capabilities, empower their positivity to pass every exam with flying colours.

# Little Blue Zen.com

www.ingramcontent.com/pod-product-compliance
Lightning Source LLC
Chambersburg PA
CBHW042356070526
44585CB00028B/2952